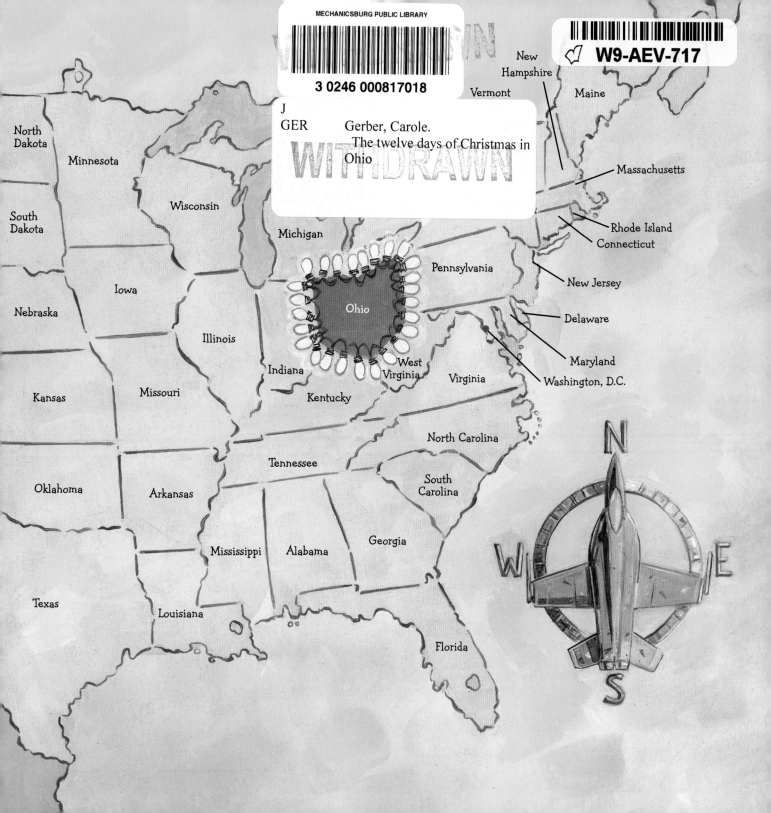

North
Dakota

Minnesota

Wisconsin

Michigan

New
Hampshire

Vermont

Maine

Massachusetts

South
Dakota

Iowa

Illinois

Indiana

Ohio

Pennsylvania

Rhode Island

Connecticut

New Jersey

Delaware

Maryland

Washington, D.C.

Nebraska

Missouri

Kentucky

West
Virginia

Virginia

Kansas

Tennessee

North Carolina

South
Carolina

Oklahoma

Arkansas

Mississippi

Alabama

Georgia

Texas

Louisiana

Florida

N

W

E

S

Michigan

Lake Erie

Toledo •
Perrysburg •
Sandusky
Fort
Meigs
Sandusky River

Cedar Point
← Amusement Park

Great Lakes
Science Center

Cleveland

• Akron

Delaware
State Park •

Holmes
County • ←
Walnut
Creek

Columbus Zoo

Ohio State
★ • University
COLUMBUS

Wright-Patterson
Air Force Base
Dayton •

Ohio &
Erie
Canal

Hocking River

Hocking
Hills State
Park

• EnterTRAINment
Junction
• Cincinnati
← Underground
Railroad Museum

West Virginia

Indiana

Pennsylvania

Kentucky

Ohio River

The Twelve Days of Christmas in Ohio

written by
Carole Gerber

illustrated by
Jeffrey Ebbeler

GOETTA

STERLING CHILDREN'S BOOKS
New York

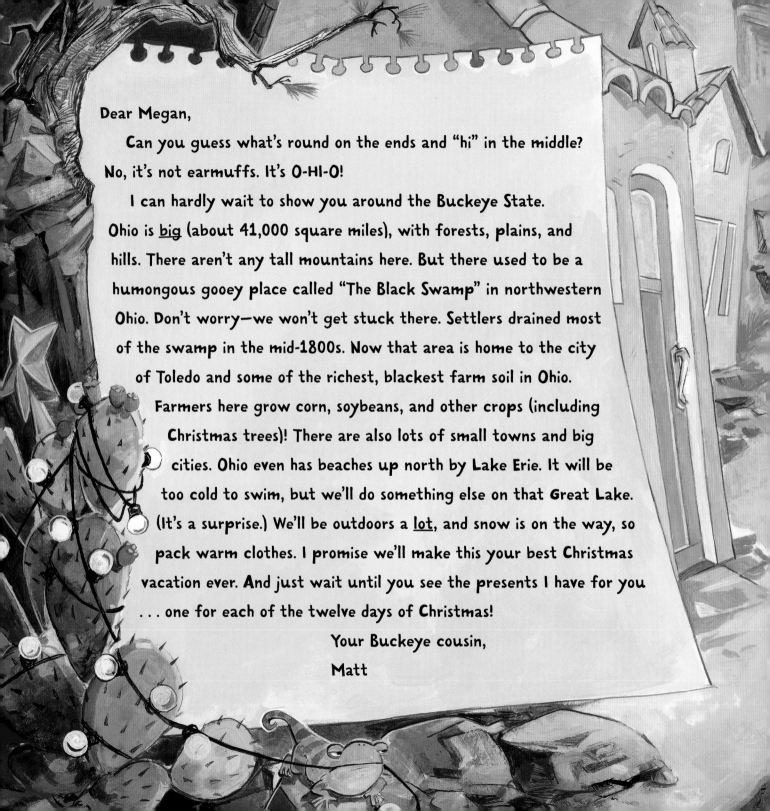

Dear Megan,

    Can you guess what's round on the ends and "hi" in the middle? No, it's not earmuffs. It's O-HI-O!

    I can hardly wait to show you around the Buckeye State. Ohio is <u>big</u> (about 41,000 square miles), with forests, plains, and hills. There aren't any tall mountains here. But there used to be a humongous gooey place called "The Black Swamp" in northwestern Ohio. Don't worry—we won't get stuck there. Settlers drained most of the swamp in the mid-1800s. Now that area is home to the city of Toledo and some of the richest, blackest farm soil in Ohio. Farmers here grow corn, soybeans, and other crops (including Christmas trees)! There are also lots of small towns and big cities. Ohio even has beaches up north by Lake Erie. It will be too cold to swim, but we'll do something else on that Great Lake. (It's a surprise.) We'll be outdoors a <u>lot</u>, and snow is on the way, so pack warm clothes. I promise we'll make this your best Christmas vacation ever. And just wait until you see the presents I have for you . . . one for each of the twelve days of Christmas!

                    Your Buckeye cousin,

                    Matt

Dear Mom and Dad,

I could see snow tumbling down outside as Matt, Aunt Lou, and Uncle Josh welcomed me at the Columbus airport. They brought GREAT gifts! Aunt Lou gave me a pair of red earmuffs and a necklace made of real buckeye nuts strung together. (Ohioans wear them at Ohio State University football games because their team is named "The Buckeyes.")

Uncle Josh has a giant sweet tooth, so he brought me a box of buckeye candy made of peanut butter dipped in chocolate. Yum! The candies look like the buckeyes that grow on Ohio's state trees.

Buckeye trees grow everywhere in Ohio, but Matt wanted to show me some special ones in Buckeye Grove on Ohio State's campus, where buckeye trees are planted to honor the school's top athletes. I pointed up at one of them and Matt whispered, "See the cardinal? It's our state bird welcoming you to Ohio." Definitely the best gift of all!

Go O-HI-O!
Megan

P.S. Here's what a buckeye looks like.

Hi, Mom and Dad,

The snow that started yesterday piled up to six inches overnight! This morning, we went snowshoeing north of Columbus in Delaware State Park. Matt hooked aluminum snowshoes to our boots and told me to copy his movements. We lifted our knees, kept our feet apart, and pushed down as we walked. It was easy!

As we crunched along—snowshoes are really noisy!—Matt explained that the area got its name from the Delaware Indians. They made <u>their</u> snowshoes from animal hides stretched over wooden frames, and wore them for winter hunting. Lots of Native American tribes once lived in Ohio. In fact, "Ohio" is the Iroquois Indian word for "great river."

We were not the only critters enjoying today's weather. Remember the cardinal we saw yesterday? He followed us! I'm SURE it's the same bird because of the little mark on his beak. I named him Red. I couldn't believe he didn't fly away when two white-tailed deer jumped in front of us! This kind of deer is Ohio's state animal and lives in all 88 counties. Matt and I decided that walking on hooves looks a whole lot more graceful than walking on snowshoes.

Crunch! Crunch!

Megan

P.S. Here's a sketch of our snowshoes.

On the second day of Christmas,
my cousin gave to me . . .

2 white-tailed deer

and a cardinal in a buckeye tree.

Brrrr! It's sunny but REALLY cold here. Good thing I brought all my winter gear because this morning we hiked through Hocking Hills State Park, tucked into the foothills of the Appalachian Mountains. We saw sandstone formations carved out 350 million years ago, giant cliffs, gorges, and waterfalls. We even got to see Ohio's biggest tree _and_ its biggest cave. And believe me, they are BIG!

Ohio's tallest tree is a 149-foot tall hemlock—nearly as tall as a 15-story building! Who knew a huge tree could be so awesome? Our next stop was Ash Cave, which is 700 feet long and has a large overhang with its own waterfall splashing down. In the _really_ old days, travelers on horseback stopped there for shelter. I wonder if they hollered to hear their voices echo back, the way Matt and I did.

Uncle Josh asked us to listen for another kind of echo. We heard a weird, low sound made by the big waterfall as it pelted against the walls of the cave. We also heard strange cooing noises. Aunt Lou said they were made by rock pigeons that nest inside the cave.

As we listened to the pigeons, I spied three little fir trees growing nearby. Matt and I decided to decorate them with whatever we could find. And guess what—the birds helped. Our cardinal even showed up!

Chirp, chirp,
Megan

Dear Mom and Dad,

We headed south toward Cincinnati today to visit two cool places. The first was "EnterTRAINment Junction," the <u>world's largest</u> indoor model train display.

There were train tracks everywhere—on the floor, spread on tables, and hanging in the air! The signs said the ninety model railroad cars were one-twenty-fourth the size of real ones. Around the tracks were tiny models of towns, forests, and teensy waterfalls with real water. I felt like a giant!

Afterward, we drove downtown to the Underground Railroad Freedom Center. Uncle Josh explained that the Underground Railroad was the name for the secret routes southern slaves followed in the 1800s as they traveled north to freedom. Those who helped them escape were called conductors because, like conductors on real railroads, they helped people travel safely.

My favorite exhibit was a collection of colorful "freedom quilts." Women sewed the quilts and hung them on their clotheslines to show runaway slaves which homes were safe places to hide.

Everyone agreed the Freedom Center was the perfect ending to our day. We were super-impressed by the courage of the slaves, and with the Ohioans who helped them escape to freedom.

Love,
Megan

On the fourth day of Christmas,
my cousin gave to me . . .

4 tooting trains

3 fir trees, 2 white-tailed deer,
and a cardinal in a buckeye tree.

Dear Mom and Dad,

If it weren't for Ohioans Orville and Wilbur Wright, I couldn't have flown to Columbus to see Matt! Today, we learned all about the Wright brothers, who grew up in Dayton, Ohio, and were "first in flight." We even saw some of the planes they built and flew in the early 1900s. Uncle Josh is a big fan of anything that flies, which is why he took us to the National Museum of the U.S. Air Force in Dayton. It's the world's biggest military flight museum, located on a huge Air Force base (Wright-Patterson), named after the Wrights and a pilot named Frank Stuart Patterson.

There's <u>so</u> much there, including 360 planes and missiles. NO way we could see it all! Uncle Josh and Aunt Lou loved the replica of the Wrights' 1909 flyer—the military's first "flying machine." Wilbur Wright even taught new pilots to fly it!

We also saw a fighter jet film at the museum's 3-D theater. This was Matt's favorite. Mine was sitting in the cockpit of a plane outfitted with an F-16 flight simulator used to train pilots. I felt brave!

Speaking of brave, the mission of the U.S. Air Force is "to fly, fight and win . . . in air, space and cyberspace." As we were leaving, some fighter jets flew over in formation. Thrilling and LOUD!

Over and out,
Megan

P.S. I've sketched the 1909 plane for you.

Hallo!

That's how some people say "hello" in Holmes County, the home of the world's largest settlement of Amish people. (Say "Ah-mish.") Their ancestors came from Switzerland, Holland, and Germany a couple of hundred years ago. Amish families still live and run their farms the old-fashioned way—no cars, no electricity, no computers! Men and boys wear plain shirts and pants with suspenders, topped by a straw hat in summer or a black hat in winter. Women and girls wear long dresses, aprons, and white caps.

They are friendly to us "English." (That's what they call people who aren't Amish.) One family even runs Walnut Creek Farm as a tourist attraction, inviting people right into their home. We toured the big house and the "dawdy" house, which is a smaller house for grandparents. We watched women sewing quilts, and a nice lady showed Matt how to thread a needle. (It took him a few tries.)

We went outside and Matt fed the horse before climbing into the buggy with me. Our buggy bumped down a winding road to an Amish bakery. We went in and stuffed ourselves with Amish cookies called "snickerdoodles." It was a yummy end to the tour.

Clip! Clop!

Megan

P.S. Here are some snickerdoodles for you to share. Don't drop any paper crumbs!

On the sixth day of Christmas, my cousin gave to me . . .

6 horse-drawn buggies

5 zooming planes, 4 tooting trains, 3 fir trees,
2 white-tailed deer, and a cardinal in a buckeye tree.

Yawn. . . .

I'm writing this letter by flashlight because I am snuggled into my sleeping bag on the shores of Lake Erie. So are Uncle Josh and Aunt Lou. But don't worry—we aren't cold! We are <u>inside</u> Cleveland's Great Lakes Science Center for a family sleepover with some other groups. None of us has ever slept in a museum or "explored" it after dark, but this is SO much fun.

Before we brought our stuff inside the museum, we toured a restored Great Lakes freighter outside. It was built in 1925, and is called "the steamship that built Cleveland" because it carried so many goods in and out of the city.

Inside the museum, we played with a bunch of interactive exhibits. Our favorites were part of the "NASA Glenn Visitor Center." We climbed into a lunar lander that had been on the actual <u>moon</u>. (Did you know "lunar" means "moon" in Latin?) We also got to see moon rocks and climb on a model of the Mars landscape. Then we slid and slipped across a digital floor projection that allowed us to "collect stars" as we hopped across the galaxy. This trip to Ohio is turning me into a science geek!

Now that it's bedtime, I have put my sleeping bag close to the lunar lander. I'll probably dream about snoozing on the moon!

Nighty-night,
Megan

On the seventh day of Christmas,
my cousin gave to me . . .

7 stars a-shining

6 horse-drawn buggies, 5 zooming planes,
4 tooting trains, 3 fir trees, 2 white-tailed deer,
and a cardinal in a buckeye tree.

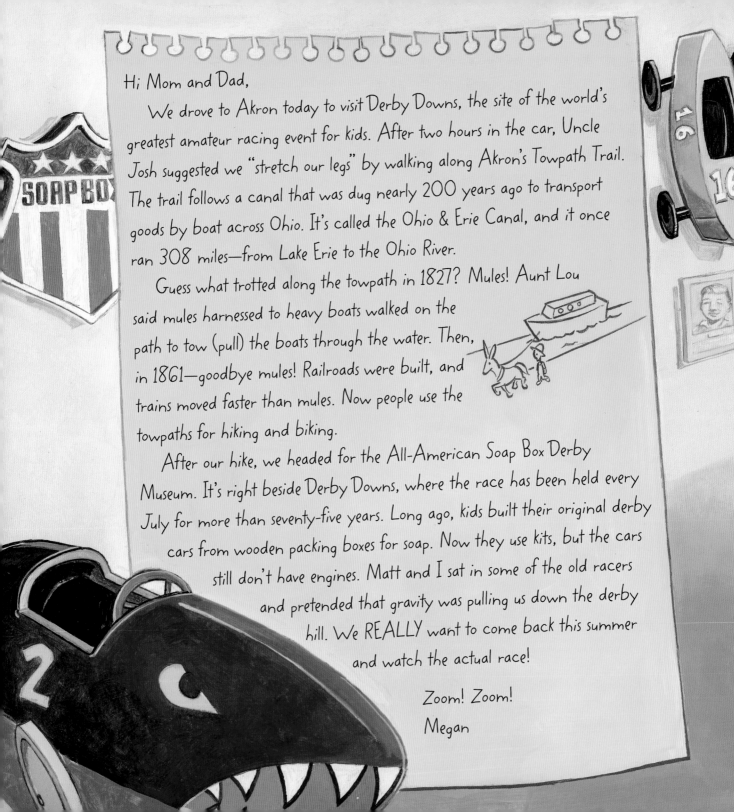

Hi Mom and Dad,

We drove to Akron today to visit Derby Downs, the site of the world's greatest amateur racing event for kids. After two hours in the car, Uncle Josh suggested we "stretch our legs" by walking along Akron's Towpath Trail. The trail follows a canal that was dug nearly 200 years ago to transport goods by boat across Ohio. It's called the Ohio & Erie Canal, and it once ran 308 miles—from Lake Erie to the Ohio River.

Guess what trotted along the towpath in 1827? Mules! Aunt Lou said mules harnessed to heavy boats walked on the path to tow (pull) the boats through the water. Then, in 1861—goodbye mules! Railroads were built, and trains moved faster than mules. Now people use the towpaths for hiking and biking.

After our hike, we headed for the All-American Soap Box Derby Museum. It's right beside Derby Downs, where the race has been held every July for more than seventy-five years. Long ago, kids built their original derby cars from wooden packing boxes for soap. Now they use kits, but the cars still don't have engines. Matt and I sat in some of the old racers and pretended that gravity was pulling us down the derby hill. We REALLY want to come back this summer and watch the actual race!

Zoom! Zoom!
Megan

On the eighth day of Christmas,
my cousin gave to me . . .

8 soap box racers

7 stars a-shining, 6 horse-drawn buggies,
5 zooming planes, 4 tooting trains, 3 fir trees,
2 white-tailed deer, and a cardinal in a buckeye tree.

Dear Mom and Dad,

Have you ever heard of "ice boating"? Me neither! But that's what we got to do today with Uncle Josh's friend Jake, who lives in Sandusky—the roller coaster capital of the world! The town's amusement park, Cedar Point, is closed in winter, but I got to see some of its <u>ginormous</u> coasters from the ice boat as we glided past on a frozen section of Lake Erie.

Erie is on the northeastern border of the U.S. and Canada and—at 240 miles long and 57 miles wide—it's the 11th largest lake in the whole world! Jake says the deepest part is toward the middle, so ice boaters stick pretty close to shore and always check to make sure the ice is completely solid before going out.

Ice boats are amazing! They look like sailboats on skis. They're wind-powered and most have only one or two seats. Because Jake's boat is so small, he took Matt and me on separate rides. He let us try steering the boat with a tiller, a stick that guides it over the ice.

Afterward, we drank hot cocoa and watched from shore as Jake raced a bunch of other ice boaters. He won first place!

Yippee!
Megan

P.S. Jake invited us back next summer to ride the roller coasters. Please say yes!

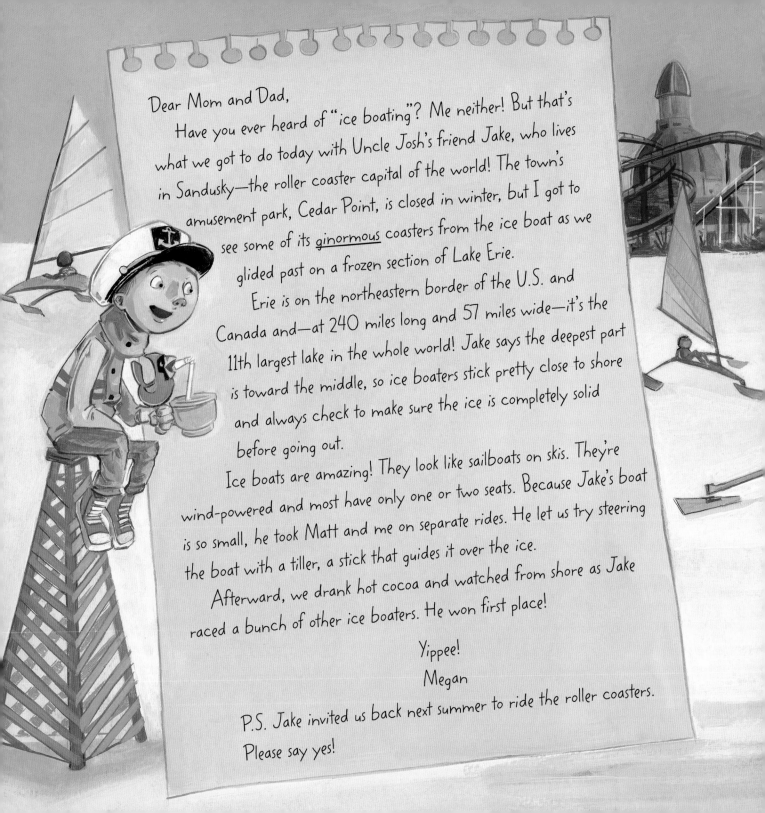

On the ninth day of Christmas,
my cousin gave to me . . .

9 gliding ice boats

8 soap box racers, 7 stars a-shining, 6 horse-drawn buggies,
5 zooming planes, 4 tooting trains, 3 fir trees,
2 white-tailed deer, and a cardinal in a buckeye tree.

Dear Mom and Dad,

Picture this: It's wintertime, it's freezing cold, and you have to build a fort. Mom, you get a pickax. Dad, you get a shovel. You'll work together to break apart the frozen ground so you can dig the fort's foundation. Good luck!

Today, at the Fort Meigs Museum in Perrysburg, we learned how 1,200 soldiers built—and then defended—a fort that protected the northwest frontier against the British during the War of 1812. Even though our country had declared its independence back in 1776, the British still wanted to control our resources and trade routes. No way!

American soldiers held off the enemy for ten days and helped to win the war. Aunt Lou says there is an Ohio history program where kids can re-enact battles and learn about soldiers' daily lives. Fun! They get to hang out in an exact replica of the actual fort, which is closed in winter. They even wash clothes by hand like soldiers did. (I'm not so sure _that_ would be fun!)

Matt and I decided to build some soldier snowmen to honor the real soldiers' bravery. We put our military hats from the museum shop on two of them, and they looked very proud!

Your snowgirl,

Megan

P.S. The American flags that flew over Fort Meigs in 1812 had only 15 stars—one for each of the first 15 states in our country.

On the tenth day of Christmas,
my cousin gave to me . . .

10 snowy soldiers

9 gliding ice boats, 8 soap box racers, 7 stars a-shining,
6 horse-drawn buggies, 5 zooming planes, 4 tooting trains, 3 fir trees,
2 white-tailed deer, and a cardinal in a buckeye tree.

Dear Mom and Dad,

When we went snowshoeing last week, Matt taught me to lift my knees, keep my feet apart, and push down. I found out the hard way that these moves do NOT work when you go ice skating! Today, we rented skates at the Ottawa Park Ice Rink, a big outdoor rink in Toledo.

Besides "open skating" for all ages, the rink hosts ice hockey games for kids. Really young players are called "squirts." We saw some of these little guys practicing as Matt led me and my wobbling ankles onto the ice.

Ice hockey is a big sport here. Toledo's pro team, the Walleyes, is named after a kind of Lake Erie fish! Matt kept me giggling—I pictured fish holding hockey sticks—as I kept my skate blades straight and learned to "step and glide." I only fell once, when I lifted my knees instead of gliding! After I got the hang of it, we took a break to watch everyone speeding around the rink. It was a great way to spend a sunny afternoon!

Your skating star,
Megan

On the eleventh day of Christmas,
my cousin gave to me . . .

11 speedy skaters

10 snowy soldiers, 9 gliding ice boats,
8 soap box racers, 7 stars a-shining, 6 horse-drawn buggies,
5 zooming planes, 4 tooting trains, 3 fir trees,
2 white-tailed deer, and a cardinal in a buckeye tree.

Dear Mom and Dad,

My last day in Ohio started and ended with a tasty surprise. This morning, Aunt Lou taught me how to make buckeye candy. Yum! Afterward, we all played an Ohio trivia game. Did you know the first traffic light was invented in Cleveland and the first pro baseball team was the Cincinnati Reds? Plus, Neil Armstrong, the first man to walk on the moon, was from Ohio!

At sunset, when the Columbus Zoo turns on millions of lights, we went to see the annual "Wildlights" display. The first thing we saw was a music and light show, where the lights seemed to leap and dance in time to the music. The animals liked it, too—we peeked at most of them as we rushed past to the other Christmas exhibits. Matt insisted the monkeys were snapping their fingers. Not!

We visited Santa's <u>live</u> reindeer, and checked out the lit-up coral reef. Guess who was there? "Diving Claus"! He was wearing a snorkel and swimming with some VERY surprised fish.

Our last holiday stop was a visit to Mrs. Claus's kitchen. She helped us decorate a dozen freshly baked sugar cookies. They were ALMOST as good as Aunt Lou's buckeye candy.

Please bring a really big truck for my Ohio goodies when you pick me up at the airport tomorrow!

Your honorary Buckeye,
Megan

On the twelfth day of Christmas,
my cousin gave to me . . .

12 Christmas cookies

11 speedy skaters, 10 snowy soldiers, 9 gliding ice boats,
8 soap box racers, 7 stars a-shining, 6 horse-drawn buggies,
5 zooming planes, 4 tooting trains, 3 fir trees, 2 white-tailed deer,
and a cardinal in a buckeye tree.

Ohio: The Buckeye State

Capital and Largest City: Columbus • **State Abbreviation:** OH • **State Bird:** the cardinal • **State Flower:** the scarlet carnation • **State Tree:** the Ohio buckeye • **State Insect:** the ladybug • **State Beverage:** tomato juice • **State Animal:** the white-tailed deer • **State Reptile:** the black racer snake • **State Motto:** "With God, all things are possible" • **State Song:** "Beautiful Ohio," music by Mary Earl; words by Ballard MacDonald and Wilbert McBride

Some Famous Ohioans:

Neil Armstrong (1930–2012), born in Wapakoneta, in 1969 was the first man to walk on the moon. A navy pilot, he became an astronaut in 1962. He flew more than 200 kinds of aircraft and in 1966 was the first to successfully dock two vehicles in space.

Thomas Edison (1847–1931), born in Milan, is best known for inventing the phonograph (1877) and perfecting the electric light bulb (1879). He held patents for 1,093 devices and substances. Among them are electric batteries and generators, and systems for distributing electric power, lights, and heat. He also helped invent the motion picture camera. Edison's inventions changed the world!

John Glenn (1921–), born in Cambridge, graduated from Muskingum College and is one of 24 Ohio-born astronauts. He was the first American to orbit the Earth (1962); in 1998 at age 77, he became the oldest person to fly in space. He also served Ohio as a U.S. senator for 25 years.

Maya Lin (1959–), a Chinese-American sculptor born in Athens, won a national design competition in 1981 to design the Vietnam War Memorial in Washington, D.C. The black stone wall lists the names of 58,272 fallen soldiers. Since then, she has created many more memorials.

Toni Morrison (1931–), born in Lorain, is an author, editor, and professor, and the first African-American woman to win the Nobel Prize in Literature. She also won the Pulitzer Prize in fiction for her novel *Beloved*.

Steven Spielberg (1947–), a Cincinnati native, is a world-famous filmmaker and producer of dozens of movies. Among them are *Lincoln*, *War Horse*, *Jaws*, and *E.T., the Extra-Terrestrial*.

Tecumseh (c.1768–1813), born near Piqua. This Shawnee Indian chief tried unsuccessfully to form an independent Indian state in the Midwest. His story is depicted every summer in an outdoor theater production in Chillicothe.

Wilbur Wright (1867–1912) and **Orville Wright** (1871–1948) were brothers who invented the first airborne plane. Wilbur was born in Millville, Indiana, and Orville was born in Dayton, Ohio. Neither earned a high school diploma, but both received honorary Ph.D. degrees from Yale and Harvard for their inventions, tested in Kitty Hawk, North Carolina, and Dayton, Ohio.

To Mark Gerber—a Minnesotan by birth, a Buckeye by choice. —C.G.

To Isabel and Olivia. —J.E.

STERLING CHILDREN'S BOOKS
New York

An Imprint of Sterling Publishing
387 Park Avenue South
New York, NY 10016

STERLING CHILDREN'S BOOKS and the distinctive Sterling Children's Books logo are trademarks
of Sterling Publishing Co., Inc.

The artwork for this book was created using acrylic paint on paper.
Designed by Ellen Duda and Andrea Miller

ISBN 978-1-4549-0890-6

Library of Congress Cataloging-in-Publication Data

Gerber, Carole.
    The twelve days of Christmas in Ohio / by Carole Gerber ; illustrated by Jeffrey Ebbeler.
        pages cm
    Summary: Megan writes a letter home each of the twelve days she spends exploring the state of Ohio at Christmastime,
as her cousin Matt shows her everything from Amish buggies to speeding ice boats. Includes facts about Ohio.
    ISBN 978-1-4549-0890-6
    [1. Ohio--Fiction. 2. Christmas--Fiction. 3. Cousins--Fiction. 4. Letters--Fiction.] I. Ebbeler, Jeffrey, illustrator. II. Title.
    PZ7.G29356Twe 2014
    [Fic]--dc23
                                                                                                                    2013040073

Distributed in Canada by Sterling Publishing
c/o Canadian Manda Group, 165 Dufferin Street
Toronto, Ontario, Canada M6K 3H6
Distributed in the United Kingdom by GMC Distribution Services
Castle Place, 166 High Street, Lewes, East Sussex, England BN7 1XU
Distributed in Australia by Capricorn Link (Australia) Pty. Ltd.
P.O. Box 704, Windsor, NSW 2756, Australia

For information about custom editions, special sales, and premium and corporate purchases, please contact
Sterling Special Sales at 800-805-5489 or specialsales@sterlingpublishing.com.

Manufactured in China
Lot #:
2 4 6 8 10 9 7 5 3 1
07/14

www.sterlingpublishing.com/kids

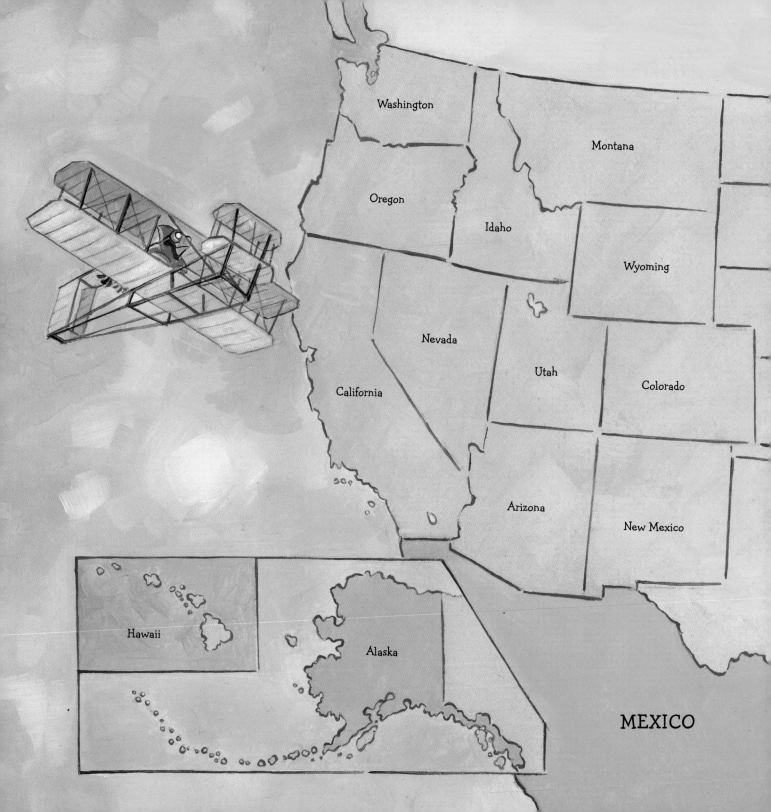